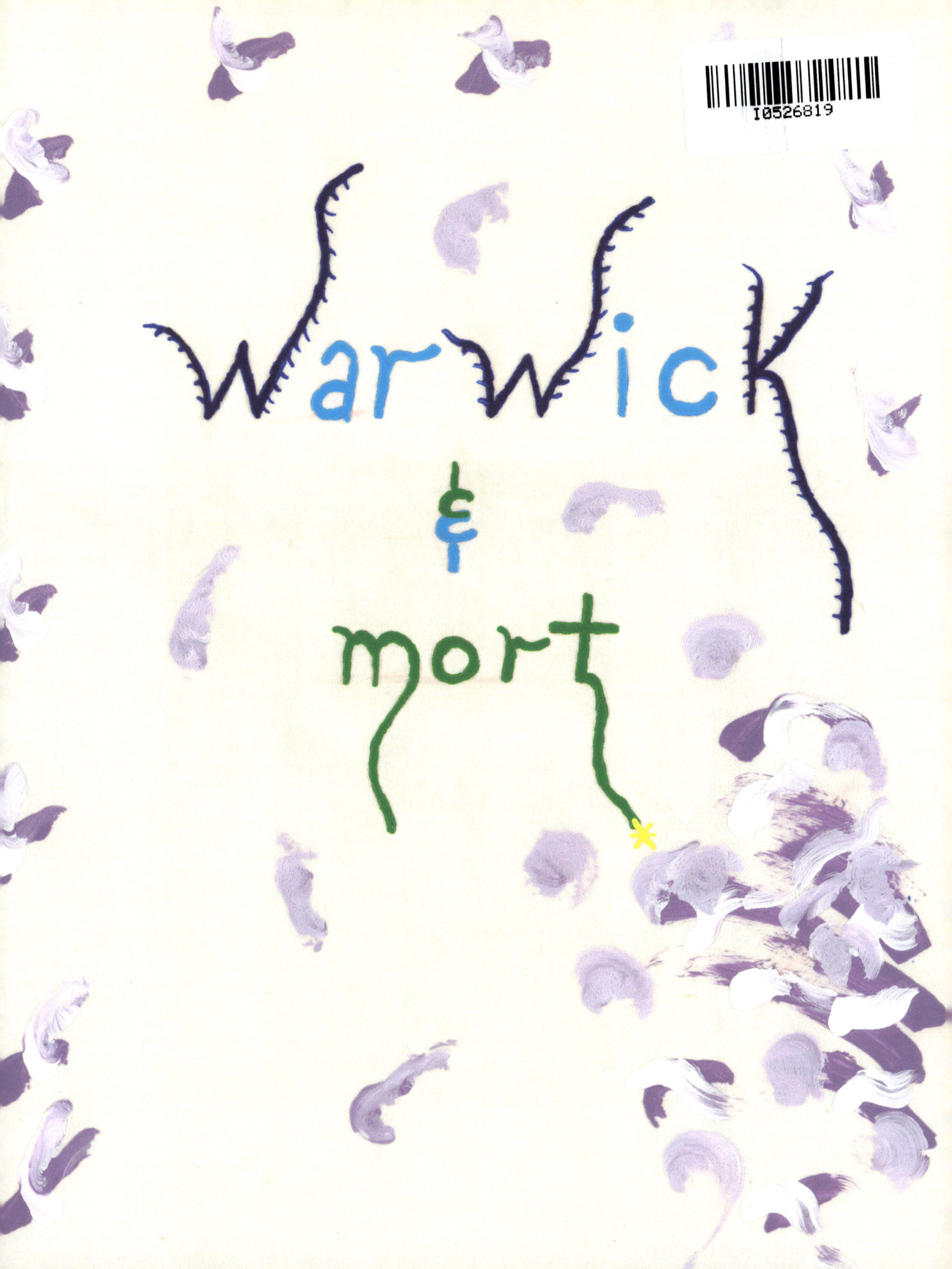

warwick & mort

ISBN   Paperback   978-1-68536-032-0
            eBook   978-1-64803-999-7

Westwood Books Publishing LLC
Atlanta Financial Center
3343 Peachtree Rd NE Ste 145-725
Atlanta, GA 30326

www.westwoodbookspublishing.com

Illustrated

created & written

by

Catherine

1

Along the sand,
near Crescent Rock;

2

a tiny boat,
with two, did dock.

In miniature marks,
of claws and shoes;

4

came ancient friends,
to cheer One's blues.

5

They set-out on
their journey far;

having heard One's
cries,
from brightest star.

Now on a quest,

to help in deeds;

they traveled

fast, to

find the

need.

A wee magician,
a dragon of blue;
as tall as your
thumb, I
swear 'tis
true.

9

They ate some
sweetmeats,
while surveying
the night;

to the owl
in the
tree,
they were
quite a
sight.

And
asking the owl, if he
knew where One lived;

12

two, went ahead on,
with full hearts
to give.

The sky was a-glitter,
sending beauty so
kind;
as Mort
climbed
the trellis,
One,
hoping to
find.

14

Wick spotted
One then,
in his bright
trundle-bed;

15

a tear on his cheek,
blankets pulled
round his head.

In sleep, the two gazed,
at a face young and bright;

then told One,
so gently,
everything was alright.

They searched round
the room,
for the
cause
of One's
troubles;

t'was, lost Teddy Bear,

in a clear
crystal bubble.

They found Ted,
unharmed,
in the toe of One's boot;

21

Teddy thanked them,
then rolled,
toward the bed,
in a
scoot.

So, Warwick and Mort,
wished the pair,
happy days;

23

then left,
as they'd come,
in a whispy
blue haze.

As the oars of a
small boat,
slapped again the
warm wet;

another One's cries,
they are answering,
I'll bet.

I'd look very closely,
when you see misty blue;

it's Warwick and Mort,
checking gently,
on you.